Asian Folktales Retold

Vietnamese Fables of Frogs and Toads

Told and Edited by Masao Sakairi

Illustrated by Shoko Kojima
Translated by Matthew Galgani

Hearing Tales as They Are Told

Do you love to listen to stories? I do. Can you listen really well?

For hundreds of years, people have passed down folktales from grandparents and parents to children by telling—not writing—them.

When people tell you a story, you don't just hear with your ears. You learn a lot from the voices the storytellers use, how they move their arms, legs, head, shoulders, and body, the expressions on their face—all the tools they use to make their tales come alive.

This book, and the others in the series Asian Folktales Retold, was created to help you truly "hear" Asian folktales and understand them deeply.

As you listen to these tales, or perhaps read them yourself when you're older, figure out for yourself what they mean. If you can hear the storyteller's voice in your head, then you are listening really well.

Published by HEIAN, P.O. Box 8208, Berkeley, California 94707
HEIAN is an imprint of Stone Bridge Press
www.stonebridge.com • sbp@stonebridge.com

Printed in China

LIBRARY OF CONGRESS CATALOGING-IN-PUBLICATION DATA

Sakairi, Masao, 1927–
　　[Katari ojisan no Betonamu minwa. English. Selections]
　　Vietnamese fables of frogs and toads / told and edited by Masao Sakairi; illustrated by Shoko Kojima; translated by Matthew Galgani.
　　　　v. cm. — (Asian folktales retold)
　　"Originally published in Japan by Hoshinowakai"—Copyright p.
　　Summary: Two Vietnamese folktales, one about a young student and his frog bride, and the other about a toad who enlists other animals to help him convince the gods to bring rain.
　　Contents: The frog bride — The toad who brought the rain.
　　ISBN-13: 978-0-89346-947-4
　　ISBN-10: 0-89346-947-5
　　1. Tales—Vietnam. [1. Folklore—Vietnam.] I. Kojima, Shoko, 1954– ill. II. Galgani, Matthew. III. Title. IV. Series.

PZ8.1.S2158Vie 2006
398.2—dc22
[E]
　　　　　　　　　　　　　　　　　　　　　　　　2006011408

The Frog Bride

Long ago, in a small village in Vietnam, there
lived a kindhearted husband and wife. But,
because they had no children, they felt sad and
lonely.

One day, they went to the riverbank to pray.

"Dear God," they said, "please help us by giving us a child."

God heard their prayer, and soon a child was born to them. But the child was not a little girl—it was a little girl frog!

"Well," the new parents said, "God has given us this child, and we must raise her with all our love and care."

Their baby girl frog quickly grew into a splendid young woman frog.

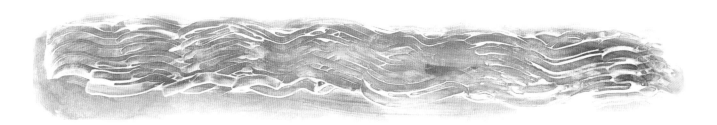

One day, the young frog announced, "Father, Mother, I've decided to marry the young man who walks by our house every day."

Now, there was, indeed, a young man who took the road in front of their house every day on his way to school. The young frog had watched him, and, as time went by, she fell in love with him.

"But, my dear daughter," said her father, "a frog can't marry a man. I've never heard of such a thing."

Still, the young frog loved the young student. So, one day, when she heard his footsteps, she hopped outside and jumped onto his shoulder.

"Please marry me," she said.

Totally surprised, the young man responded, "Wait a minute—you're a frog! How come you can talk?"

"Yes, I'm a frog, but my mother and father are human. I can do any kind of work, so please take me to be your bride."

The young man was astonished, but he took a liking to this highly unusual frog, and after thinking it over he decided that he would, indeed, like to marry her.

When the young man arrived home that day, his aged mother was waiting for him.

"Mother," he announced, "I've decided to marry a frog—a young girl frog who can talk. I know it's surprising, but I believe she is a blessing from God, for there's never been any creature so rare in the world. Please come with me to her house."

His mother went with him to the frog's home, and there they discussed the young couple's marriage, but the young man's mother was upset.

"A young man marrying a frog? That's ridiculous! Don't do it! If you want to marry, why not marry a young student?"

Still, the young man stuck to his decision. He just set the frog on his shoulder and left her house. When they reached his own home, the frog jumped off his shoulder and hopped into the house. Then the two got married right there.

Bright and early the next morning, the young husband found a delicious breakfast ready and waiting for him. It had a wonderful aroma like no other and a flavor you would have to taste to believe. His frog bride was in fact a master chef.

When the young man went to school and told his friends that he had married a frog, they laughed and laughed.

"Just how down and out do you have to be to marry a frog?" they teased him. Then they plotted, "Let's play a trick on him. Let's put his frog bride to the test."

The next day, when the young man arrived at school, a classmate told him with a serious face, "There's a ceremonial feast tomorrow at our teacher's house. We need to bring the food, so have your wife cook something, all right?"

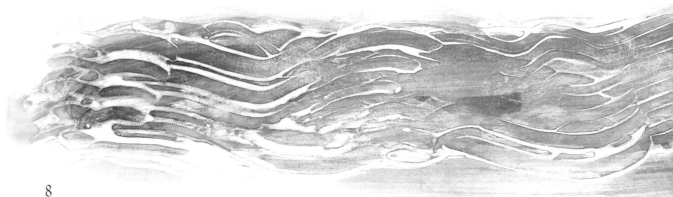

Arriving home after school, the young husband found that his house was spotless, as usual, and his frog bride was waiting for him with a smile. But he sat down looking worried.

"Is something wrong?" his wife asked.

"Yes, actually," he admitted. "I need to prepare some food for a ceremonial feast at my teacher's house, and I don't know how. Frogs don't know anything about cooking for ceremonial feasts, do they? That's what's bothering me."

"Now, now, don't you worry about a thing," the frog bride assured him, giggling happily. "I'll make you something. Just sit back and relax. Maybe read a book."

The next day, the young man was able to bring his teacher an astounding feast. The teacher was amazed at the unexpected ceremonial dinner and overjoyed at the food the young man had brought. His classmates were, too. "We've never seen anything like this. Who could have made it?"

"My wife made it, of course," said the young man.

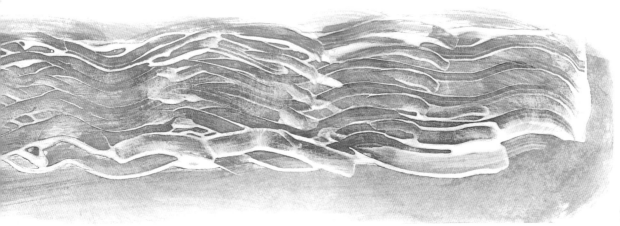

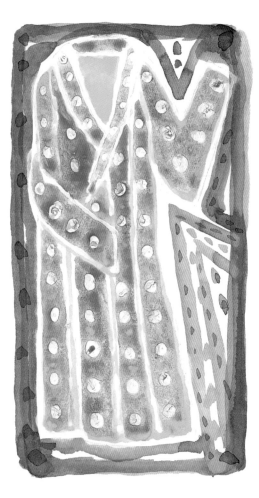

Since their trick had failed, the classmates decided to test the frog bride with something even more difficult—surely a frog wouldn't be able to sew, they thought. They told the young man, "We need to make some fine new clothes as a birthday present for our teacher. Have your wife make some, won't you?"

Once again, the young man was troubled and returned home with a long face.

"Is something wrong?" asked his bride.

"Yes, actually," he admitted. "I need to make some fine new clothes for my teacher as a birthday present, and I don't know how. Frogs don't know anything about sewing fine clothing, do they?"

"Now, now, don't you worry about a thing," the frog bride assured him, giggling happily. "I'll make you something. Just sit back and relax. Maybe read a book."

The next day, the young man was able to bring a set of beautiful clothes to his teacher's birthday party. The teacher was amazed at the unexpected gift and overjoyed at the clothes the young man had brought. His classmates were, too. "We've never seen anything like these. Who could have made them?"

"My wife made them, of course," said the young man.

Once again, the trick had failed to make fun of and embarrass the young man who had married a frog. So, the classmates all decided they needed to see this frog bride. "Everyone's invited to our teacher's house to welcome the new year," they told the young man, adding, "Wives, too."

"There's no way to get out of this one," thought the young man. His classmates were sure to make fun of him if he brought his frog bride. He wondered what to do. "No matter how talented or smart she is, a frog is still a frog," he said to himself. "If everyone sees with their own eyes that I've really married a frog, they'll make fun of me so much that I won't want to go to school anymore."

The troubled young man headed home with a long, sad face.

"Is something wrong again?" asked his worried bride.

"No, nothing," he said. "We're invited to my teacher's house to celebrate the new year."

By the time New Year's Day came, the young man had decided he would just quit school after the party and live peacefully with his frog bride, for he truly loved her with all his heart.

So, he placed her on his shoulder and headed out to his teacher's house. Along the way, the frog bride jumped off his shoulder and hopped into the forest, telling him, "You go ahead. I'll catch up with you later."

But the young man stood where he was and watched his wife.

In the forest, the frog bride slipped off the frog skin she'd been wearing. (I have no idea how she did that!) She emerged as a beautiful woman.

It turned out that she had taken the form of a frog, but the bride was, in fact, a woman all along.

She hid the frog skin in the shade of a tree. But the young man had seen the whole thing, so he found the frog skin right away. He ripped it up, and threw it away. Then he took the hand of his bride.

"Now that the skin is destroyed, I can't go back to being a frog," said his wife. "Because you're such a good man, God gave you a wife. And because I met such a kind man, I was allowed to become a woman again."

The young man's classmates were already gathered at the teacher's house for the party. They were eager to see his frog bride and make fun of him for marrying her.

But two *people* arrived. Wow, were the students surprised!

"What a fine-looking young couple!" they exclaimed. And, can you imagine what happened? At the sight of the bride and groom, the students' meanness disappeared, and they blessed the pair instead of ridiculing them.

The young man and his beautiful bride lived happily ever after.

The Toad Who Brought the Rain

Long, long ago, in an old pond in an old forest, there lived a toad.

At that time, Vietnam was suffering from a terrible drought—it hadn't rained for months and months. Little by little, all of the water in the toad's pond dried up, leaving the bottom dry and cracked.

The leaves fell from the trees in the forest, and the animals went here and there looking for water to drink. It was a terrible time.

"This is awful," thought the toad. "I'll soon die if it doesn't rain. Croak, croak. What should I do? Croak."

Then, suddenly, he croaked, "I have an idea. I'll ask the gods in the heavens to help."

In the heavens, there was a garden, and from there the gods watched over the earth. The toad left his dry pond, and began to walk to the heavens, his feet sticking with each hop and croak.

"Hey there, Toad," a crab called out. "Where are you off to in this drought?"

"Hello, Crab," Toad replied. "I'm going to ask the gods to make it rain."

"That's a great idea! Rain is just what we need. I'll go with you."

So Crab and Toad went off together.

Along the way, they met a tiger and a bear.

"Hey there, Crab and Toad," they said. "Where are you two going in this drought?"

"Hello, Tiger and Bear. We're going to ask the gods to make it rain."

"That's a great idea! Rain is just what we need. We'll go with you."

So Tiger, Bear, Crab, and Toad went off together.

After they left the forest and reached the fields, they came across a fox and some honeybees.

"Hello, Toad, Crab, Tiger, and Bear," they said. "Where are you going in this drought?"

"Hello, Fox and Honeybees. We're going to ask the gods to make it rain."

"That's a great idea! Rain is just what we need. We'll go with you."

So off they all went on their long, hard journey.

At last, they came to the gate of the garden in the heavens.

"Now, I have a plan," said Toad. "Everybody hide. Crab, you hide in the pitcher. Honeybees, you hide under the gate. Bear, Fox, and Tiger, hide where you can, and be very quiet. Whatever you do, don't roar."

Toad then marched up to a large drum at the gate. He boldly
banged on the drum. Boom! Boom! Boom!

From inside the garden, the God of Lightning appeared.

"Who dares to beat my drum?" he thundered. "Show yourself."

Toad froze. But the God of Lightning saw him. "Send out the chicken to catch this creature who has the nerve to disturb me," he ordered.

"Now's your chance," Toad called to Fox. Fox leapt out from his hiding place and quickly caught and ate the chicken.

Then the gods sent out a dog to catch Fox.

"Now's your chance," Toad called to Bear. Bear quickly caught and killed the dog.

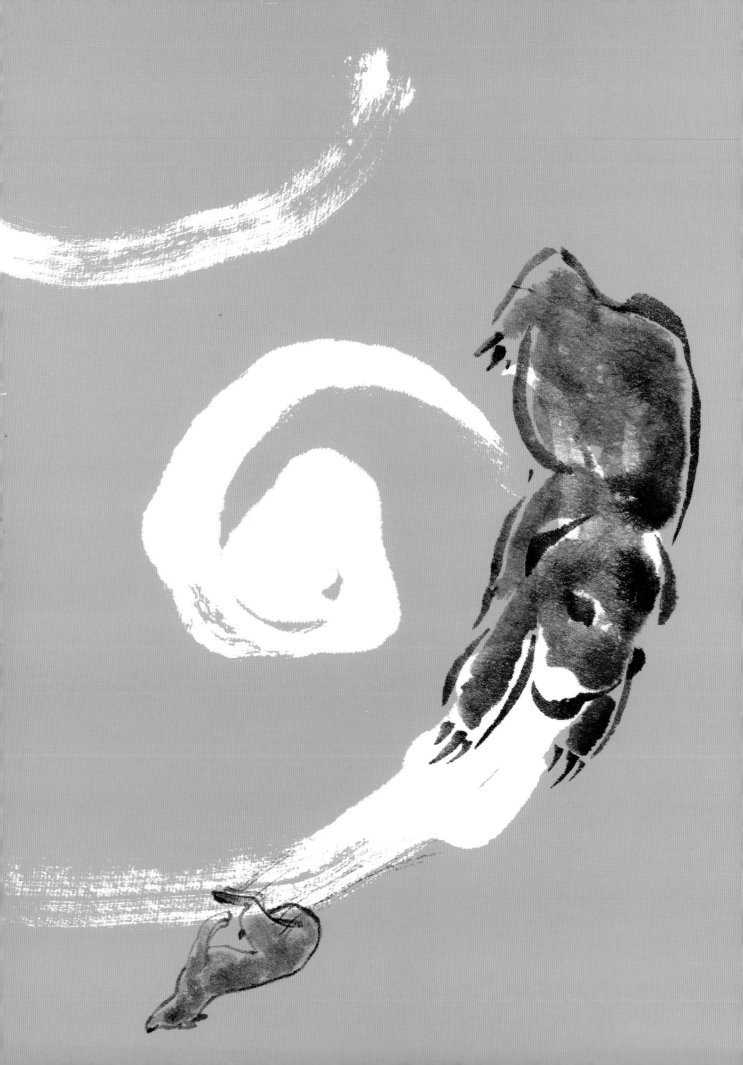

Then the gods sent the God of Lightning to catch the bear.

"Now's your chance," said Toad to the honeybees and the crab.
The bees stung the God of Lightning and the crab pinched him.

"Ouch! Ow, ow! Ouch!" cried the God of Lightning as he tried to
get away from them.

"Now's your chance," said Toad to Tiger.
Tiger then pounced on the God of Lightning and ate him.

Surprised by Toad's success against all these enemies, the Chief God himself came to the gate.

Toad hopped up to him. "I beg of you, most powerful god, please shower us with rain. The ponds and rivers are all dry. The animals and trees and plants are all dying. Please make it rain."

Bear, Tiger, Honeybees, Fox, and Crab all begged and pleaded for rain, too.

"I see, I see," said the Chief God. "OK, I shall make it rain."

Then he told Toad, "Listen, my shrewd little fellow, if you ever have dry days again, come close to the heavens and make your croaking sound. That will be a signal to remind me to make it rain."

So, the Chief God made rain fall onto the earth, as he had promised. And ever since that day, you can always hear toads croaking before it rains.

About the Series and This Book

The Asian Folktales Retold series was created to capture the spirit of Asian folktales and give them new life, showing children how these stories help us both evaluate the modern world and connect with a rich cultural past. The stories strive to preserve the oral flavor of recountings of tales passed down for generations, and they are intended to be read aloud to experience the full joy of this picture book.

The Vietnamese folktales in this book are told by Masao Sakairi, a storyteller active in the Shibuya Folktale Association of Tokyo. His style of storytelling is to unveil the tale and its imagery slowly, so that the children listening have time to respond. Sakairi manifests the wisdom that comes with age, great powers of persuasion, and the skills of a fine teacher in his storytelling.

When Sakairi retired from his teaching career, he became a volunteer for the Association for Aid and Relief, Japan, helping refugees learn Japanese and adjust to life in Japan. Among his students were some of the 8,000 Vietnamese refugees living in Japan, and Sakairi learned several folktales from them.

In the summer of 1997, folktale researcher Keiko Nomuro was approached in Niigata Prefecture by a Vietnamese woman who had a copy of the book *Philippine Folktales*, which Nomura had edited. The woman asked if there was a similar book of Vietnamese folktales. She was a Vietnamese refugee in Japan and wanted to read Vietnamese folktales to her child. She knew that other mothers like her, who had fled their country in time of war and were still feeling the effects, had an unabated longing for their homeland.

The encounter led Nomuro to approach Masao Sakairi and ask him to retell some of the Vietnamese folktales from his repertoire for a children's book. As the project progressed, the editors were also fortunate to get assistance from Gwen Tai An, a Vietnamese exchange student at Kitazato University, where Sakairi was teaching Japanese, who retold some modern Vietnamese folktales for this collection.

Miyoko Matsutani, executive consultant for the series, provided invaluable input and guidance. The many refugees who contributed stories deserve the publisher's sincere gratitude for being part of the creation of this book.

About the Storyteller and Editor

Born in Tokyo in 1927, Masao Sakairi devoted his career to teaching Japanese to junior high school students, until he retired in 1993. Then Sakairi got involved with refugees, through the Association for Aid and Relief, Japan (AAR Japan). He volunteered to teach Japanese to refugees from Vietnam and other nations, as well as to people of Japanese descent who had been left behind and raised in China after World War II. Sakairi currently volunteers as a teacher of Japanese to Vietnamese exchange students. He has collected Vietnamese folktales and is a leader of the Shibuya Folktale Association, engaged in storytelling and working with the elderly to preserve Japan's own oral traditions.

About the Illustrator

By illustrating this book, artist Shoko Kojima wanted to send children everywhere a message from Vietnam. In preparation, she traveled throughout Vietnam taking photos to capture the strength and resilience of a people who had survived war and adversity. Her illustrations of animals and natural landscapes beautifully embody the heart and soul of the Vietnamese people.

Born in 1954, Kojima graduated from the fine arts department of the Tokyo National University of Fine Arts and Music. Although she focuses on individual exhibits, she has also illustrated countless publications. A professional artist and a mushroom fanatic, Kojima lives with her dog, cat, and killifish and enjoys life in the great outdoors.

Asian Folktales Retold Series

Executive Consultant   Miyoko Matsutani
Executive Editor   Keiko Nomura

About Vietnam

Vietnam is located on the eastern side of the Indochina Peninsula at the southern border of China, with Laos and Cambodia sharing the peninsula to the west. It is about the size of New Mexico, but has over 80 million people! This long, narrow land in the shape of an S is entirely in the tropical zone, with temperatures generally between 80 and 100 degrees. Vietnam's river valleys, coastal deltas, and highland plateaus are fertile food-growing areas; the mountains provide forests and mineral deposits. Rice, rubber, and coal are the main products.

Legend has it that the first Vietnamese were descendants of a dragon lord and a heavenly spirit. There is evidence of prehistoric settlers in the region by 12,000 B.C.E., but recorded history begins about 2,700 years ago. For more than 1,000 years, from 207 B.C.E. to 939 C.E., Vietnam was ruled by Chinese dynasties. It constantly struggled for independence, and sometimes managed to throw out the Chinese for a few years. After the Vietnamese won lasting independence in 939, they were ruled by a series of dynasties. But internal warring battered the country, splitting the north and the south in the sixteenth and seventeenth centuries.

Vietnam suffered greatly over the next two centuries, first under domination by French colonialists and then as a battleground in World War II. The war between North and South Vietnam that lasted from 1954 to 1975 brought more heartache to the Vietnamese people as bigger nations—France, the United States, the Soviet Union, and China—used the conflict as a surrogate for their own power struggles. Vietnam is now unified as the Socialist Republic of Vietnam. Although its long history of war is not easily forgotten, Vietnam today is improving its relations with its neighbors and strengthening its economy.

Farming, especially rice cultivation, is still important in Vietnam, and the landscape is dotted with green fields and villages. Hanoi in the north, with 3 million residents, is the capital and cultural center and is known for its many lakes. Ho Chi Minh City in the south has 5 million people and is a commercial and industrial center with major port facilities on the Saigon River. Fifty-four ethnic groups make up the Vietnamese population, creating a diverse culture of different languages, customs, and cuisines.

Other Books from Heian

Asian Folktales Retold

as told by Miwa Kurita

illustrations by Saoko Mitsukuri

The first two volumes in this series each contain two lively Chinese tales. 32 pages in full color, 10" x 12", hardcover with dust jacket. Juvenile Fiction / Folktales. Each volume $16.95.

China Tells How the World Began
How the World Began, Why Cats Hate Rats.
ISBN 0-89346-944-0.

Chinese Fables Remembered
The Brothers and the Birds, The Two Rooster Friends.
ISBN 0-89346-945-9.

Japanese Fairy Tales

by Keisuke Nishimoto

illustrations by Yoko Imoto

Each volume in this series contains five or more classic Japanese fairy tales, with brief introductory notes about each tale. 32 pages in full color, 10" x 12", hardcover with dust jacket. Juvenile Fiction / Folktales. Each volume $14.95.

Vol. 1: The Old Man who made the Flowers Bloom, Mouse Wrestling, Kitty's New Vest, Kintaro, The Crane's Gift. ISBN 0-89346-845-2.

Vol. 2: The Straw Millionaire, The Contest, The Bouncing Rice Ball, The Monkeys' Statue, Little One Inch Boy, Tail Fishing. ISBN 0-89346-849-5.

Vol. 3: The Shining Princess, The Goblin's Fan, Peach Boy, The Cat's Dance, The Stone Statues. ISBN 0-89346-929-7.

Vol. 4: The Monkey and the Crab, The Gold Coin Drying Field, Gonbei the Duck Hunter, The Cat and Crab Race, Urashimataro. ISBN 0-89346-930-0.